Boys Are Witches Too!

Words and Drawings by Ted Enik   Colors by Shiloh Penfield

Type set in Little Trouble/Minion/Times

ISBN: 978-0-7643-6823-3
Printed in China

Copublished by Pixel Mouse House & REDFeather Mind, Body, Spirit
An imprint of Schiffer Publishing, Ltd.
4880 Lower Valley Road
Atglen, PA 19310
Phone: (610) 593-1777; Fax: (610) 593-2002
Email: Info@redfeathermbs.com
Web: www.redfeathermbs.com

Written by Beth Roth and Ted Enik ❋ Illustrated by Ted Enik

A cauldron full of "Thanks" to Beth Roth
for her indispensable help in jump-starting this project.

Wee Witches

We're All Witches

Picture a person practicing Witchcraft. You probably right away thought of a woman (maybe old and ugly; one hopes not) tossing yukky things into a bubbling cauldron, but the female-only thing is only pretty recent. Early on, "witch" was actually a verb; it described something one did, not who one was.

We now know that the terrible Witch Trials in Europe and colonial America were, for the most part, the way that important and cruel men (politician, judges, priests) held on to power. The Bible says Eve ruined everything, so women and girls were automatically "trouble." As mothers and family healers, they were more in touch with Nature's ways than men and so were said to "believe" in something other than the one, all-powerful, father God.

In the 1960s, women fighting for equal rights created same-sex safe spaces where males wouldn't try to take charge. This naturally led to female-only Covens (a group of practicing Witches), and many exist today. But, from ancient times till now, Witchcraft has always welcomed both women and girls, and men and boys.

"Wizard" or "Witch"? Which is it? We can trace the word "Wizard" to the 14th century. But language scholars suggest that its meaning may echo even farther back to a term of respect for someone who has lived a long and full life. We still use the word "wizened" to describe the wrinkled face of the elderly.

And as for "Warlock?" Best avoid the word altogether.
A person who snitched on a Witch, which led to prison or hanging? That was a Warlock. A male Witch who leaked the secrets and rituals of a Coven? Again, a Warlock. Hundreds of years ago, Warlock was incorrectly used by the church to insult and condemn ordinary male Witches. From there it jumped into RPGs, books, and movies, where it's still used a lot.
Has anybody read these "Henry Potter" books?

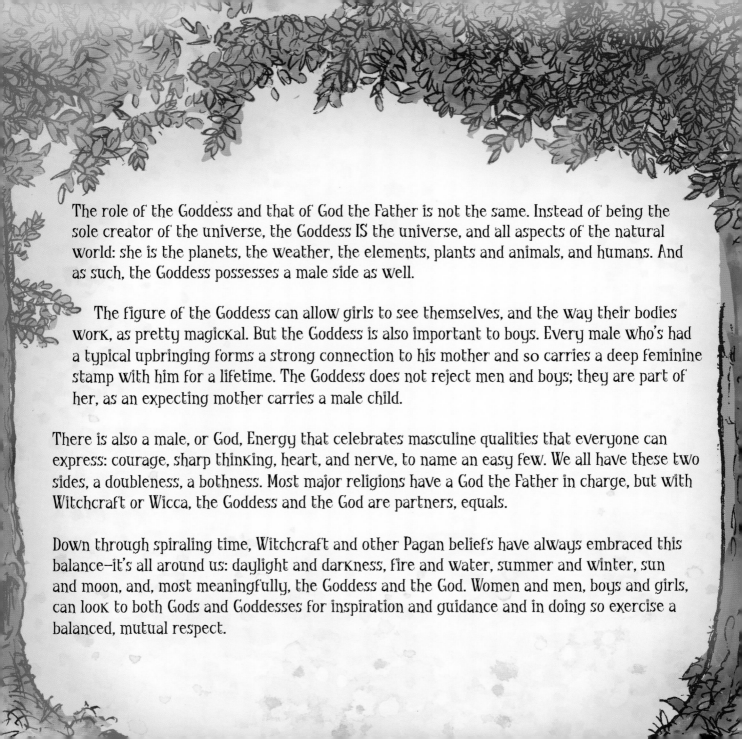

The role of the Goddess and that of God the Father is not the same. Instead of being the sole creator of the universe, the Goddess IS the universe, and all aspects of the natural world: she is the planets, the weather, the elements, plants and animals, and humans. And as such, the Goddess possesses a male side as well.

The figure of the Goddess can allow girls to see themselves, and the way their bodies work, as pretty magickal. But the Goddess is also important to boys. Every male who's had a typical upbringing forms a strong connection to his mother and so carries a deep feminine stamp with him for a lifetime. The Goddess does not reject men and boys; they are part of her, as an expecting mother carries a male child.

There is also a male, or God, Energy that celebrates masculine qualities that everyone can express: courage, sharp thinking, heart, and nerve, to name an easy few. We all have these two sides, a doubleness, a bothness. Most major religions have a God the Father in charge, but with Witchcraft or Wicca, the Goddess and the God are partners, equals.

Down through spiraling time, Witchcraft and other Pagan beliefs have always embraced this balance—it's all around us: daylight and darkness, fire and water, summer and winter, sun and moon, and, most meaningfully, the Goddess and the God. Women and men, boys and girls, can look to both Gods and Goddesses for inspiration and guidance and in doing so exercise a balanced, mutual respect.

A When Mom cuts an Apple
In half it exposes
A secret for Witches,
Right under our noses!

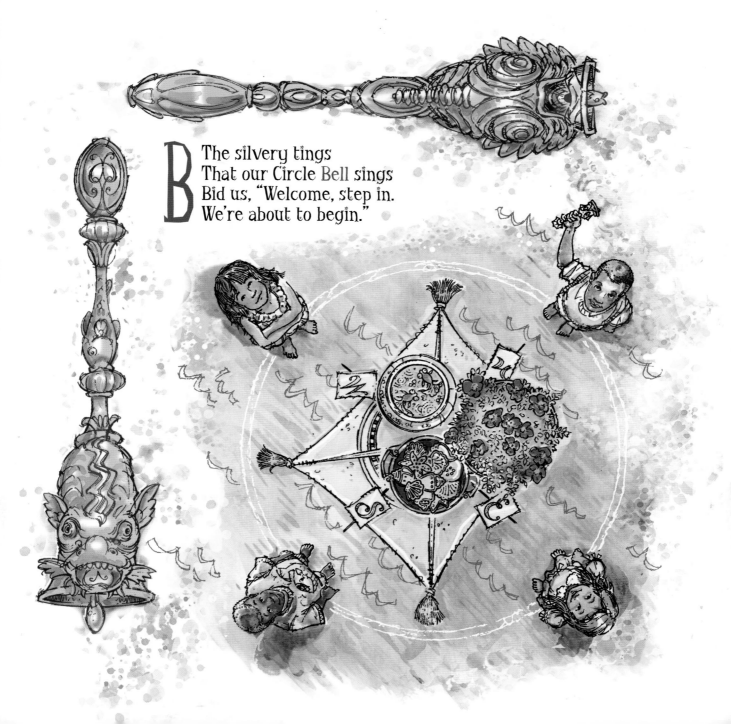

B The silvery tings
That our Circle Bell sings
Bid us, "Welcome, step in.
We're about to begin."

This **Chrysalis** holds
An unfolding surprise.
Look! A moon moth emerges
And flutterbye-byes.

D The sun and the moon
Playing tag overhead
Turns the Dawn into Dusk—
I'm not ready for bed!

E We sit 'round the bonfire,
Our faces alight,
And listen to wisdom
The Elders recite.

The Forest is crisscrossed
With moss-covered trails.
I like to imagine
A highway of whales.

Say, "Oh, Gee!" for Geode.
You never would guess
That this everyday rock
Held such wonderfulness.

H A Hare in the meadow
Encircled by mist,
Waits still as a stone
For Persephone's kiss.

Intention means giving
A wish a head start;
It's a map from your mind
And a path from your heart.

J A Jar is a wishing well;
Glass, how it gleams!
Trade jelly and pickles,
For beetles and dreams.

K My grandma's old tackle box
Smells like the sea.
I can lock away worries
By turning the Key.

L Corn mother, Demeter—
In August, at Lammas—
Invites us to greet her
In harvest pajamas.

Hi, Moon! Luna Mama!
I see you rose early.
To soak up some sunbeams,
All ghostly and pearly.

N The Narwhal is known as
A "sea unicorn."
Can't think of the reason ...
I'm teasing! His HORN!

O The woodland is rocking
With knocking and creaks.
These are voices of Ogham,
The language of trees.

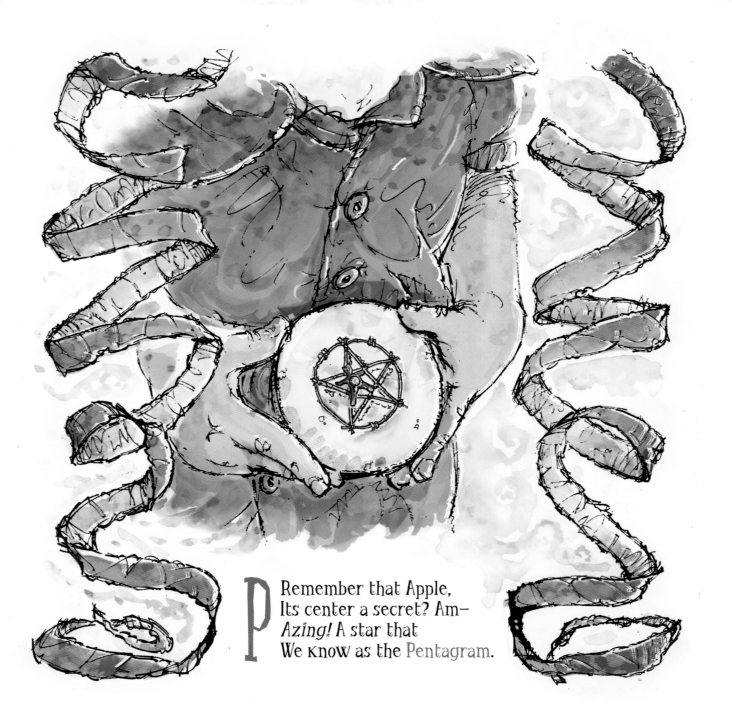

P Remember that Apple,
Its center a secret? Am—
Azing! A star that
We know as the Pentagram.

The Quarters are compass points,
Elements, seasons.
Our Circle has corners
For magical reasons.

R Witches' Familiars are
Only their pets. And
The woods have a Raven,
She eats from my hand.

S

You know about Salem;
Those terrible trials.
It's Halloween Town now,
Year 'rounded by smiles.

T Mama Moon tells the Tide
"Life is wide! Go and play!
Just remember, come in
At the end of the day."

U When things are Uncanny,
They're hard to define:
Unexplained wonders that
Tingle your spine.

V On All Hallows Eve—
It's a witchy belief—
That the Veil between worlds
Grows as thin as a leaf.

W The clock hands tick backward,
The sunrise unwritten.
That way is called Widdershins—
So is our kitten!

X An X on the eyes
Of a dumb cartoon cat
Means its 9 lives are gone.
"You're a ghost now, so SCAT!"

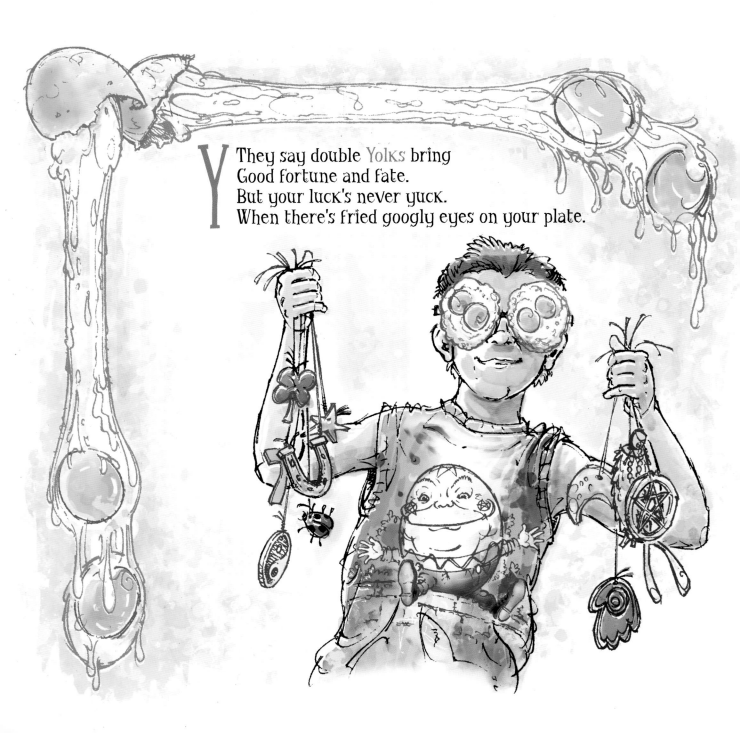

They say double Yolks bring
Good fortune and fate.
But your luck's never yuck.
When there's fried googly eyes on your plate.

The night sky is jeweled
With objects and creatures—
The Signs of the Zodiac;
Oracles, teachers.

Author-illustrator Ted Enik is probably best known as the primary artist for the popular Fancy Nancy "I Can Read™" series. In addition, he channeled Hilary Knight for the canonical hardcover *Eloise in Hollywood*. Throughout, Ted has been a writer—plays and film—and now illustrated books and graphic novels with quirky plots and original voices, often à la Dr. Seuss. You can find most of his published work by searching "Ted Enik" on the following websites:

https://www.schiffer-kids.com
https://redfeathermbs.com
http://pixelmousehousebooks.com

Shiloh's previous work includes *Boy Zero* for Caliber Comics, a guest artist spot on *Red Knight*, published by Dead West Comics, independent projects, and all four of Brian Wray's Schiffer Kids books, including the award-winning *Unraveling Rose*, and *The Bravest Knight Who Ever Lived* by Daniel Errico, which served as the basis for the HULU animated series. She is located in Brooklyn, where her calico cat "Maki" maintains quality control and ensures all pages are delivered on time.

https://www.overdrive.com/creators/1066486/shiloh-penfield